1/2019

W1

TABLE OF CONTENTS

Want to take your research further? Ask your librarian if your school subscribes to PebbleGo Next. If so, when you see this helpful symbol 🔍 throughout the book, log onto www.pebblegonext.com for bonus downloads and information.

LOCATION

Minnesota sits at the center of the long border between the United States and Canada. North Dakota and South Dakota lie to the west. Iowa is on the south. Wisconsin and Lake Superior line Minnesota's eastern edge. Minnesota's capital, St. Paul, lies on the east bank of the Mississippi River. Minneapolis, St. Paul, and Rochester are Minnesota's largest cities.

PebbleGo Next Bonus!
To print and label your own map, go to www.pebblegonext.com and search keywords

4

Minneapolis is one of Minnesota's Twin Cities.

GEOGRAPHY

Lakes, forests, and prairies are found across Minnesota. Lake Itasca in the northern part of the state is where the Mississippi River begins. The Mississippi River is the largest river in the country. Forests cover much of Minnesota. Some of the state's forests are in the Boundary Waters Canoe Area and in Voyageurs National Park. Rolling prairies cover the southern half of Minnesota. In northeastern Minnesota, the rocky Superior Upland region lies near Lake Superior. To the east is Minnesota's highest point, Eagle Mountain. It is 2,301 feet (701 meters) above sea level.

PebbleGo Next Bonus!
To watch a video about Duluth, go to www.pebblegonext.com and search keywords:
MN VIDEO

Boundary Waters Canoe Area is over 1 million acres (404,690 hectares) in size and serves as part of Minnesota's border to Canda.

There are 11,842 lakes in Minnesota that are 10 acres (4 hectares) or larger.

Scale

Miles
0   30   60   90   120

0   30 60 90 120 150
Kilometers

Red River of the North

Lake of the Woods

Voyageurs National Park

Upper Red Lake

Eagle Mountain ▲

Lower Red Lake

SUPERIOR UPLAND

St. Louis River

Lake Itasca

Leech Lake

Lake Superior

Mississippi River

Mille Lacs Lake

St. Croix River

Bois de Sioux River

YOUNG DRIFT PLAINS

Minnesota River

DRIFTLESS AREA

Mississippi River

DISSECTED TILL PLAINS

N
W   E
S

Legend

▲	Highest Point
⬭	Lake
▢	National Parks and Monuments
∿	River

WEATHER

Minnesota has cold winters and hot, humid summers. The average January temperature is 8 degrees Fahrenheit (minus 13 degrees Celsius). The average July temperature is 70°F (21°C).

Average High and Low Temperatures (St. Paul, MN)

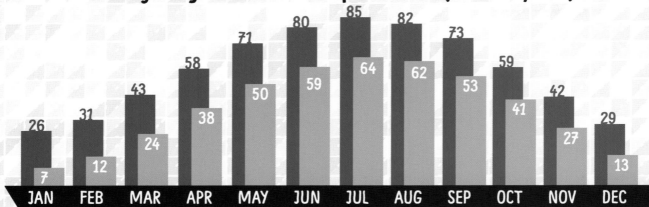

	JAN	FEB	MAR	APR	MAY	JUN	JUL	AUG	SEP	OCT	NOV	DEC
High	26	31	43	58	71	80	85	82	73	59	42	29
Low	7	12	24	38	50	59	64	62	53	41	27	13

Mall of America

The Mall of America in Bloomington is the largest indoor shopping center in the United States. The mall boasts more than 520 stores and attracts 40 million visitors each year.

Minneapolis Sculpture Garden

The Minneapolis Sculpture Garden is located across from the Walker Art Center in Minneapolis. It is the largest urban sculpture garden in the nation. It features more than 40 works, including the huge Spoonbridge and Cherry sculpture.

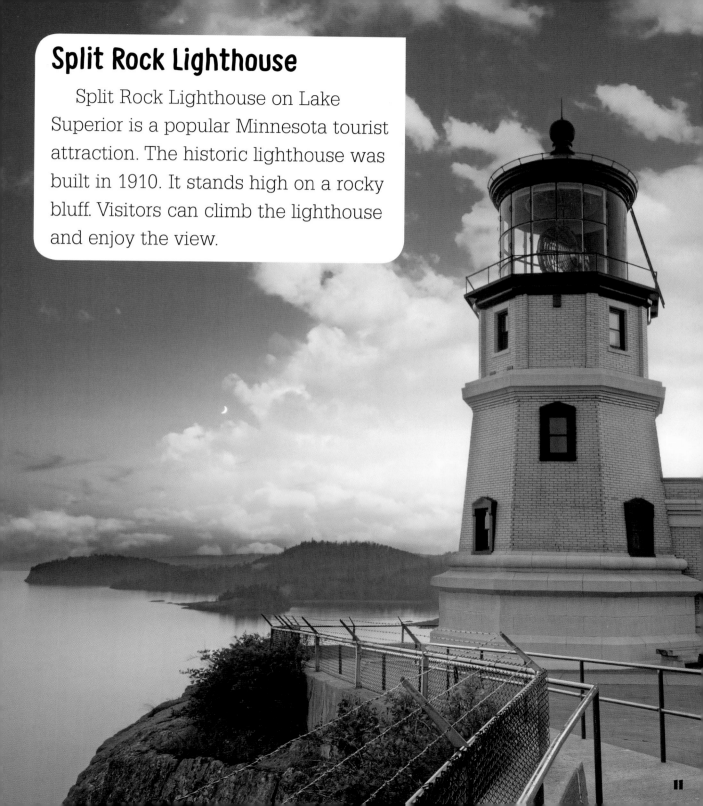

Split Rock Lighthouse

Split Rock Lighthouse on Lake Superior is a popular Minnesota tourist attraction. The historic lighthouse was built in 1910. It stands high on a rocky bluff. Visitors can climb the lighthouse and enjoy the view.

HISTORY AND GOVERNMENT

The Ojibwe and Dakota Indians were the first to settle in Minnesota. Today, there are 11 different Indian tribes across the state.

In the 1600s the Dakota and Ojibwa Indians lived in what is now Minnesota. French explorers came to the area in 1659. Great Britain won eastern Minnesota from France in 1763. After the Revolutionary War (1775–1783), the United States received eastern Minnesota from Great Britain. In 1803 the United States bought a large area of land, including western Minnesota, from France. The sale was called the Louisiana Purchase. Through the years, parts of Minnesota belonged to several different territories. In 1849 Minnesota Territory was formed. In 1858 Minnesota became the 32nd state.

Minnesota's government has three branches. The governor leads the executive branch, which carries out laws. The legislature consists of a 67-member Senate and a 134-member House of Representatives. The legislature makes the laws. Judges and their courts make up the judicial branch. They uphold the laws.

Fort Snelling was the first European settlement in Minnesota.

INDUSTRY

Service industries are the largest part of Minnesota's economy, making up about 80 percent of the state's employment. Hotels and travel agencies, health services, childcare services, and libraries are all service industries.

Minnesota is one of America's top farming states. Farms cover more than half of Minnesota's land. Farmers grow corn, soybeans, sugar beets, hay, and wheat. They also raise hogs, dairy cattle, and beef cattle.

Food products are Minnesota's top manufactured product. The state produces

Corn is Minnesota's top-produced crop.

meat and dairy products, frozen foods, and canned fruits and vegetables. Minnesota workers make computers, agricultural and construction machinery, and medical equipment.

Mining is one of Minnesota's oldest industries. The Mesabi Range in northern Minnesota has the nation's largest iron-ore deposits.

Iron is mined from the Hull Rust-Mahoning open pit mine in Hibbing.

POPULATION

White people are the largest population group in Minnesota. More than 4 million Minnesotans are white. African-Americans form the second-largest ethnic group. Many African-Americans have come to the state since the 1940s. Today more than 260,000 African-Americans live in the state. About 250,000 Hispanics also reside in Minnesota. Asians began moving into the state in the late 1900s. Hmong came in the 1980s from Laos, Vietnam, and Thailand. In the late 1990s and early 2000s, many Somalis left their war-torn country in Africa and moved to Minnesota.

Population by Ethnicity

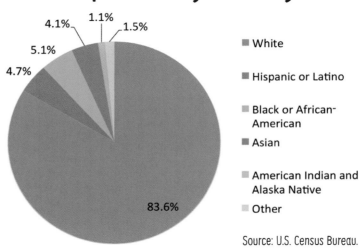

4.1%
1.1%
1.5%
5.1%
4.7%
83.6%

- White
- Hispanic or Latino
- Black or African-American
- Asian
- American Indian and Alaska Native
- Other

Source: U.S. Census Bureau.

FAMOUS PEOPLE

Prince Rogers Nelson (1958–) is a rock music star. He is known as "Prince." His albums include *Purple Rain*, *Sign "O" the Times*, *20Ten,* and *HITnRUN*. Prince was born in Minneapolis.

Jesse Ventura (1951–) has been a professional wrestler, actor, and talk show host. He served as the governor of Minnesota from 1999 to 2003. He was born in Minneapolis.

Laura Ingalls Wilder (1867–1957) wrote *Little House on the Prairie* (1935) and many other books about pioneer life. *On the Banks of Plum Creek* (1937) is based on her life in Walnut Grove. Wilder was born in Wisconsin.

Walter Mondale (1928–) represented Minnesota in the U.S. Senate from 1964 to 1976. He was the U.S. vice president under President Jimmy Carter (1977–1981). He ran for president in 1984 but lost. His running mate was Geraldine Ferraro, the first woman chosen as a vice-presidential candidate. He was born in Ceylon.

F. Scott Fitzgerald (1896–1940) wrote stories about America's Jazz Age — the 1920s. *The Great Gatsby* (1925) is one of his most famous novels. He was born in St. Paul.

Sinclair Lewis (1885–1951) was an author whose novels attacked the weaknesses he saw in U.S. society. In 1930 he became the first American to win the Nobel Prize for literature. He was born in Sauk Centre.

STATE SYMBOLS

Tree

Norway pine

Flower

pink and white lady's slipper

Bird

common loon

Fish

walleye

PebbleGo Next Bonus! To make Minnesota's state muffin, go to www.pebblegonext.com and search keywords: **MN RECIPE**

Mushroom

morel

Grain

wild rice

Animal

white-tailed deer

Muffin

blueberry muffin

Fruit

honeycrisp apple

Gemstone

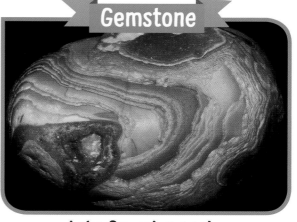

Lake Superior agate

FAST FACTS

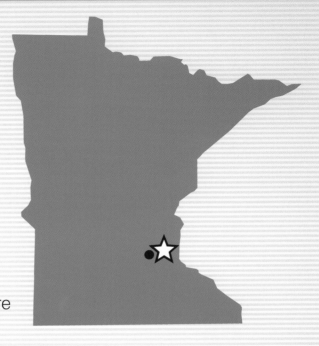

STATEHOOD
1858

CAPITAL ☆
St. Paul

LARGEST CITY •
Minneapolis

SIZE
79,627 square miles (206,232 square kilometers) land area (2010 U.S. Census Bureau)

POPULATION
5,420,380 (2013 U.S. Census estimate)

STATE NICKNAME
The Gopher State, Land of 10,000 Lakes, and the North Star State

STATE MOTTO
"L'Étoile du Nord," which is French for "The Star of the North"

STATE SEAL

The Minnesota seal stands for the state's government. The seal shows a farmer near Saint Anthony Falls. The farmer is plowing a field near a stump. He stands for Minnesota's farming and logging industries. Nearby, an American Indian on horseback represents Minnesota's first people. The state motto, "L'Étoile du Nord" appears above them. The motto is French for "The Star of the North."

PebbleGo Next Bonus! To print and color your own flag, go to www.pebblegonext.com and search keywords:

MN FLAG

STATE FLAG

Minnesota's state flag is royal blue with gold fringe. The state seal is in the center of the flag. The seal shows a farmer plowing a field, the falls of St. Anthony, and an American Indian riding a horse. Minnesota's motto, "The Star of the North," appears in French on the seal. Around the seal is a wreath of lady's slippers, the state flower. Three dates appear on the wreath. One is 1819, the year U.S. soldiers arrived. The second is 1858, the year Minnesota became a state. The third is 1893, the year the flag was adopted. The 19 stars around the wreath symbolize that Minnesota was the 19th state to join the Union after the original 13. The largest star stands for Minnesota.

MINING PRODUCTS

iron ore, sand and gravel, granite

MANUFACTURED GOODS

computers and electronic equipment, petroleum and coal products, food products, fabricated metal products, machinery, chemicals, paper, printed material, plastics and rubber products

FARM PRODUCTS

dairy, soybeans, corn, wheat, wild rice, hogs, beef cattle, sugar beets

PROFESSIONAL SPORTS TEAMS

Minnesota Timberwolves (NBA)

Minnesota Lynx (WNBA)

Minnesota Twins (MLB)

Minnesota Vikings (NFL)

Minnesota Wild (NHL)

PebbleGo Next Bonus!
To learn the lyrics to
the state song, go to
www.pebblegonext.com
and search keywords:

MN SONG

MINNESOTA TIMELINE

1600 — Dakota and Ojibwa Indians live in the area that is now Minnesota.

1620 — The Pilgrims establish a colony in the New World in present-day Massachusetts.

1659 — French explorers Pierre Esprit Radisson and Médard Chouart des Groseilliers are the first Europeans to come to Minnesota.

1763 — Great Britain wins eastern Minnesota from France.

1775–1783 — American colonists fight for their independence from Great Britain in the Revolutionary War.

1783 Eastern Minnesota becomes U.S. territory.

1803 The United States buys a large area of land, including western Minnesota, from France. The sale is called the Louisiana Purchase.

1820 Construction of Fort Snelling begins. It becomes Minnesota's first permanent European settlement.

1849 Minnesota Territory is created by Congress.

1858 Minnesota becomes the 32nd U.S. state.

1861–1865

The Union and the Confederacy fight the Civil War. More than 24,000 Minnesotans fight for the Union.

1863

Soldiers of the 1st Minnesota Regiment lead an attack on the Confederacy at the Battle of Gettysburg. The Union wins the battle. But the Minnesota Regiment loses 215 of its 262 soldiers.

1890

The country's largest iron-ore deposits are discovered in the Mesabi Range in northeastern Minnesota.

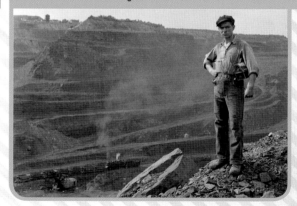

1914–1918

World War I is fought; the United States enters the war in 1917.

1939–1945

World War II is fought; the United States enters the war in 1941.

1965

Hubert Humphrey, a U.S. senator for Minnesota, becomes U.S. vice president under President Lyndon B. Johnson.

1977

Walter Mondale, a U.S. senator for Minnesota, becomes U.S. vice president under President Jimmy Carter.

1992

The largest U.S. mall, Mall of America, opens in Bloomington.

1998

Former professional wrestler Jesse Ventura is elected governor of Minnesota, becoming the first Reform Party candidate in the country to win a statewide office. In 2000 Ventura left the Reform Party to become an independent.

2007

A section of the Interstate 35W bridge across the Mississippi River in Minneapolis collapses, killing at least 13 people and injuring about 100 people.

2014

The Mayo Clinic, based in Rochester, celebrates its 150th year. The Mayo Clinic is one of the world's largest medical centers.

2015

Minnesota becomes the second state to create a Military Spouses and Families Day to honor the support and sacrifices made for the betterment of the country.

Glossary

attract *(uh-TRAKT)*—to get the attention of someone or something

bluff *(BLUFF)*—a tall, steep bank or cliff

employment *(em-PLOI-muhnt)*—the work someone does for salary or wages

ethnic *(ETH-nik)*—related to a group of people and their culture

executive *(ig-ZE-kyuh-tiv)*—the branch of government that makes sure laws are followed

industry *(IN-duh-stree)*—a business which produces a product or provides a service

judicial *(joo-DISH-uhl)*—to do with the branch of government that explains and interprets the laws

legislature *(LEJ-iss-lay-chur)*—a group of elected officials who have the power to make or change laws for a country or state

novel *(NOV-uhl)*—a book that tells a long story about made-up people and events

petroleum *(puh-TROH-lee-uhm)*—an oily liquid found below the earth's surface used to make gasoline, heating oil, and many other products

urban *(UR-buhn)*—having to do with a city

Read More

Brill, Marlene Targ. *Minnesota.* The Land of 10,000 Lakes. It's My State! New York: Cavendish Square Publishing, 2015.

Ganeri, Anita. *United States of America: A Benjamin Blog and His Inquisitive Dog Guide.* Country Guides. Chicago: Heinemann Raintree, 2015.

Higgins, Nadia. *What's Great About Minnesota?* Our Great States. Minneapolis: Lerner Publications Company, 2015.

Internet Sites

FactHound offers a safe, fun way to find Internet sites related to this book. All of the sites on FactHound have been researched by our staff.

Here's all you do:

Visit *www.facthound.com*

Type in this code: 9781515704102

Critical Thinking Using the Common Core

1. The Mississippi River is the longest river in the country. Where does it begin? (Key Ideas and Details)

2. Which Minnesota governor was a former professional wrestler? (Key Ideas and Details)

3. Novelists F. Scott Fitzgerald and Sinclair Lewis were born in Minnesota. What is a novel? (Craft and Structure)

Index